Maree Dundee

The Adventures of
Henry & Penny-
Carnegie Castle
Book 2

The Adventures of Henry & Penny-Carnegie Castle
BOOK 2

iUniverse books may be ordered through booksellers or by contacting:

iUniverse
1663 Liberty Drive
Bloomington, IN 47403
www.iuniverse.com
844-349-9409

ISBN: 978-1-6632-6395-7 (sc)
978-1-6632-6396-4 (e)

Library of Congress Control Number: 2024912610

Print information available on the last page.

iUniverse rev. date: 07/15/2024

Dedication

To my husband.

Thank you for providing this wonderful opportunity. Your leap of faith made it happen.

To my three children.

Thank you for embracing the adventure of an international move. Your tenacity, determination, humility and humor are admirable. You encountered many changes and yet you simply got on with it and seized each day resulting in many marvelous achievements.

To Henry & Penny,

When you arrived in the USA, the family circle was complete. You are forever loved and will never be forgotten.

"Crikey, Penny, can you believe we are going to America? Mickey Mouse, Donald Duck, and Pluto!" I was so excited. I just wanted to get out of this crate and out of this big white bird!

We seemed to have been in the big metal bird a very long time; the roar of the engines actually put me to sleep for a little while. It felt like we were floating among the clouds. Penny and I lay right up against the side of the yellow and red crates so that we could feel each other's fur. I found that very comforting because I hated being in the crate on my own. Penny and I did everything together!

My tummy did a big flip-flop as the metal bird seemed to dip down a little. The noise of the engines grew quiet, and then my tummy flip flopped again.

"Wake up, Pen; I think we are going to stop soon."

There was a loud *whooshing* sound and then a *screechy* noise followed by a *bump*. After that, we rolled along slowly, once again on the ground. I stood up and stretched and tried to see in the dark.

Eventually the metal bird stopped, and the door opened, letting in the bright sunshine. After being in the dark for so long, I had to blink and blink to see where I was. My eyes watered and burned after being in the metal bird for so long.

An enormous man with a big black beard peered in the doorway. The next minute he was towering over our crates. He had very hairy arms and hands as big as paddles; his eyes crinkled as he smiled down at us.

"Hello, you two; welcome to the United States. What a long journey you have had!"

With that, he lifted our crates one at a time onto the moving belt. The crates clattered along and then plopped off the end of the belt.

7

7

At the end of the belt, another man lifted our crates into the back of a van and drove a short distance before stopping.

He reached into the back of the van and put leads on our collars. "Come on, you two; I bet you want to stretch your legs after such a long journey." He then took us inside a fence and took the leads off our collars.

"Away you go—run, little guys, and get some fresh air." Penny and I ran around, enjoying the soft grass under our feet; it sure was great to get outside and run around. We ran and jumped and rolled around together, scratching our backs on the grass.

After a little while the man called us to come back and get our leads on. We have been taught good manners by our mum and dad, so we did as we were asked, had the leashes attached, and were then led back to the van and put back in the crates.

9

"And away we go! The next stop is the boarding kennel," said the man.

Boarding kennel? I thought. *What about our family? Where are Mum and Dad? Where are the kids?* I bet they were missing us as much as we were missing them. It seemed like such a long time since we had been snuggling with little Lea or had gone on a walk with our family.

A short while later, we arrived at a large white building that looked like a castle, with beautiful gardens and grass all around it. There was even a pretty fountain in the front courtyard that had a dog statue on the top.

"Welcome to Carnegie Castle for dogs!" said a roly-poly lady with the curliest hair I have ever seen. "You are going to be treated like a king and queen for a few days until you get used to being in another country."

As she spoke, her curls bounced and bounced around her face, which looked really funny. I had to try very hard not to burst out laughing at her!

King and queen—now you're talking, I thought. I knew poodles were like kings, and I knew I was regal. It was about time my good breeding was recognized! King Henry certainly had a nice ring to it!

We went into a room where there were several other dogs, all shapes and sizes. They were all in different crates with soft and snuggly beds to lie on. A few tails wagged, and most looked kind.

"Now I think your mummy said that you like to crate together, so I will put you in one big crate. It says here you also like a bone to chew and squeaky toys to play with. Here you go, two toys and two bones for you. Settle in, my little dears, as it will soon be playtime."

"Pen, can you believe how soft this bed is?" I asked.

"Henry, I am so thankful to be in the same crate as you. I was quite scared when I was alone. I never ever want to be separated from you again," said Penny.

We chewed away at our bones, which were a delicious chicken flavor, and then tossed a squeaky toy around between us. If only I knew where our family was, things wouldn't be too bad!

A short while later, the same lady came and let us out of the crate, along with all the other dogs. We went through a big door and out onto the grass. There were toys everywhere, a small swimming pool, ramps to run up and down, and things to jump over. There was even a tunnel to run through, which looked like great fun.

The biggest dog I have ever seen looked down at me and wagged his tail. I later found out he was a great Dane named Hercules. He was huge and had very kind eyes.

Penny and I ran and jumped and made friends with all the other dogs; everyone was nice and the barking rang out into the beautiful sun-kissed morning.

I really missed my family but quickly realized that Carnegie Castle was not too bad. Everyone was kind, the food was great, and we had a lovely soft bed to sleep on. And best of all, Penny and I were together so we could snuggle!

After four days, following playtime, Penny and I were taken in for a bath.

Now, I had never been fond of getting wet, and I absolutely detested the hairdryer. The problem was, my poodle hair had to be dried and brushed, or I ended up looking like white steel wool.

Penny loved having a bath and even stood still while she got a ribbon put in her hair. I felt foolish, but the hairdryer really scared me. I just had to close my eyes and hope that it would be finished soon. I tried counting bones, but then I decided to try to think about our old house in Australia and just wait for the ordeal to be over.

The next morning, we said goodbye to all our new friends. One by one, they all gave us a nuzzle or a lick, and then it was time to be loaded into the van again.

"Penny, where do you think we are going now?"

It seemed such a long time since we had seen our human family. I missed them so much, but I figured everyone we had met so far was kind and caring. Surely everything would work out okay! I wondered what adventure tomorrow would bring.

About the Author

Maree grew up in a dusty and hot Australian town in the state of Victoria. As a child, she loved to read and expand her horizons outside of her small town. She met her husband whilst traveling in France and quickly moved to Sydney-a big exciting city!

Adventure, fun, 3 children, and multiple pets followed.

Maree wanted to share the experience of her children growing up in Australia, the beautiful landscape, the wildlife, and the adventures they all experienced.

Her first book- "Kassie the Kookaburra" tells a tale of friendship and laughter and showcases the beautiful setting of the family home in Bonnet Bay, Sydney.

Maree is thrilled to now present "The Adventures of Henry & Penny" which is a four-book series.

These delightful books detail the journey of these two beloved dogs from Australia to the USA and the many new things they encounter along the way.

Throughout the books, you will get to hear about what Henry and Penny saw and did on their exciting and at times hilarious journey toward their new life in America!

Printed in the United States
by Baker & Taylor Publisher Services